Editor: Ellen Turnbull
Cover and interior design: Verena Velten
Illustrations: Marlene McBrien

SILVER
FSC CERTIFIED   BIBLIOGRAPHIC DATA 2008-09

CopperHouse is an imprint of Wood Lake Publishing, Inc. Wood Lake Publishing acknowledges the financial support of the Government of Canada, through the Book Publishing Industry Development Program (BPIDP) for its publishing activities. Wood Lake Publishing also acknowledges the financial support of the Province of British Columbia through the Book Publishing Tax Credit.

At Wood Lake Publishing, we practise what we publish, being guided by a concern for fairness, justice, and equal opportunity in all of our relationships with employees and customers. Wood Lake Publishing is committed to caring for the environment and all creation. Wood Lake Publishing recycles, reuses, and encourages readers to do the same. Resources are printed on 100% post-consumer recycled paper and more environmentally friendly groundwood papers (newsprint), whenever possible. A percentage of all profit is donated to charitable organizations.

Library and Archives Canada Cataloguing in Publication

Giuliano, David, 1960-
        The alligator in Naomi's pillow / David Giuliano ; illustrated by Marlene McBrien.
ISBN 978-1-55145-586-0
        I. McBrien, Marlene, 1965- II. Title.
PS8613.I845A65 2010   jC813'.6   C2010-902194-0

Published by CopperHouse
An imprint of Wood Lake Publishing Inc.
9590 Jim Bailey Road, Kelowna, BC, Canada, V4V 1R2
www.woodlakebooks.com
250.766.2778

Printing 10 9 8 7 6 5 4 3 2 1
Printed in Canada by Transcontinental

the Alligator in Naomi's Pillow

David Giuliano

Illustrated by Marlene McBrien

CopperHouse

In the middle of the night Naomi screamed. "EEEEE!"
She ran down the hall to her parents' bedroom.
She jumped on their bed and kept screaming, "EEEEEE!"

Naomi's dad bounced two feet straight up in the air.
He grabbed the alarm clock on the way up.
He read it on the way back down.

Naomi's mom said, "Hmgu bib?"

Naomi said, "An alligator came out of my pillow. She wants to bite me on the neck!

"What do you want us to do?" asked Naomi's mom.

Naomi thought about it.

"I want you to beat the alligator up."

So Naomi's mom got out of bed. They went down the hall to Naomi's room. She couldn't find the alligator. So she beat Naomi's pillow up. She punched it. She jumped on it. She drop kicked it across the room.
Then they all went back to bed.

But in the middle of the *next* night, Naomi screamed, "EEEEEE!"
She ran down the hall to her parents' bedroom.
She jumped on their bed and kept screaming, "EEEEEE!"

Naomi's dad bounced *three* feet straight up in the air.
He grabbed the alarm clock on the way up.
He read it on the way back down.

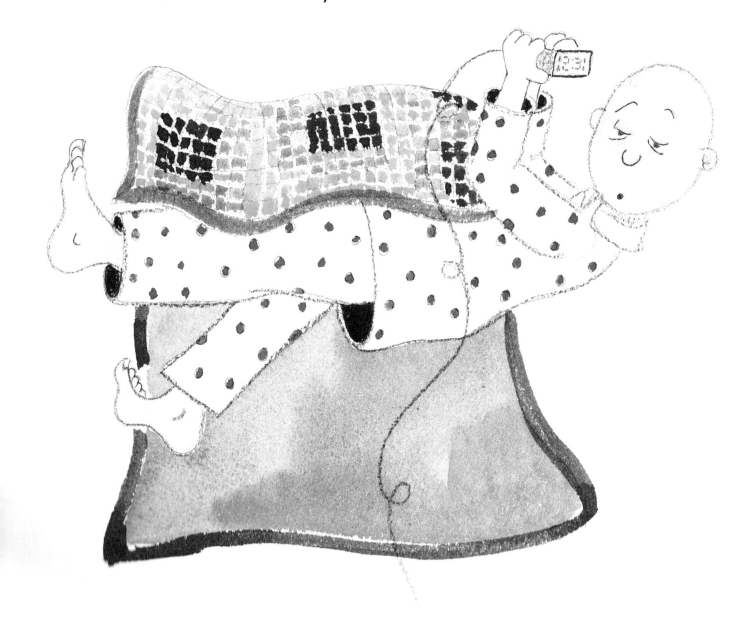

Naomi's mom said, "Hmgu bib?"
Naomi said, "The alligator is back.
She wants to bite me on the neck!"

"What do you want us to do? asked Naomi's dad.

Naomi thought about it.

"I want to trade pillows with you."

So Naomi's dad took his pillow.
He went down the hall to Naomi's room.
He couldn't find the alligator.
So he traded pillows with Naomi.
Then they all went back to bed.

But in the middle of the *next* night
Naomi screamed, "EEEEEE!"
She ran down the hall to her parent's bedroom.
She jumped on their bed and kept screaming,
"EEEEEE!"

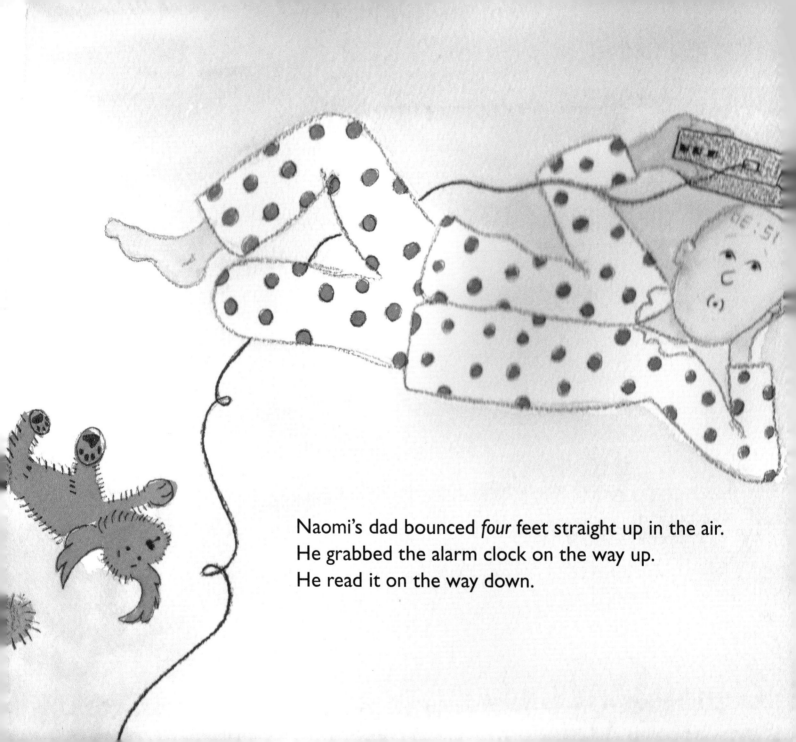

Naomi's dad bounced *four* feet straight up in the air.
He grabbed the alarm clock on the way up.
He read it on the way down.

Naomi's mom said, "Hmgu bib?"

Naomi said, "The alligator is back. She wants to bite me on the neck!"

"What do you want us to do?" asked Naomi's mom and dad.

Naomi thought about it.

"I don't know."

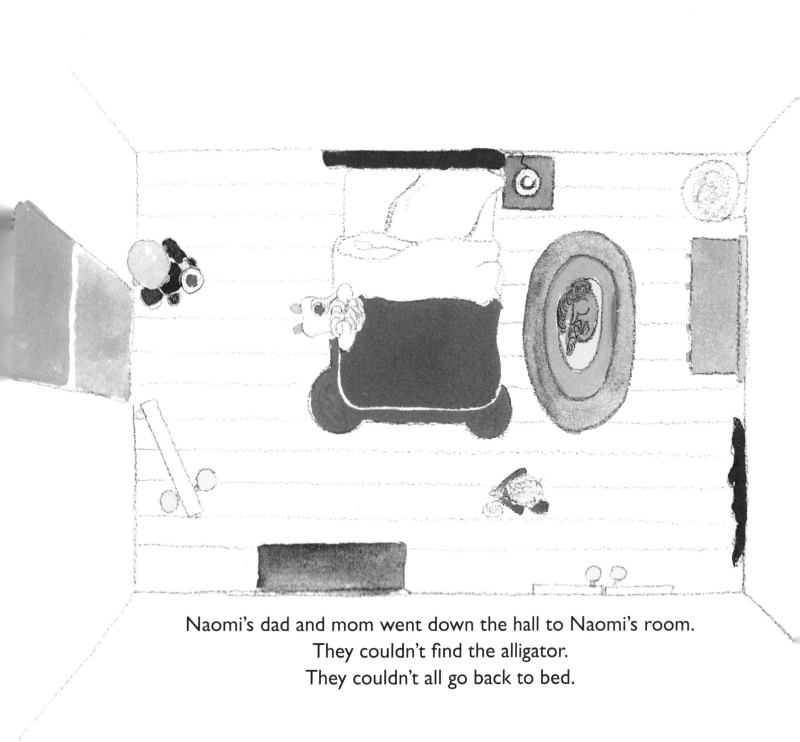

Naomi's dad and mom went down the hall to Naomi's room.
They couldn't find the alligator.
They couldn't all go back to bed.

"How do you know there *is* an alligator?" asked her dad.
Naomi rolled her eyes. "I saw her!"

"How do you know she wants to bite your neck?" asked her mom.

"I don't know," said Naomi.

"Maybe you should ask the alligator if she *really* wants to bite your neck," said Dad.

Naomi put her hands over her neck.
She leaned down near her pillow.

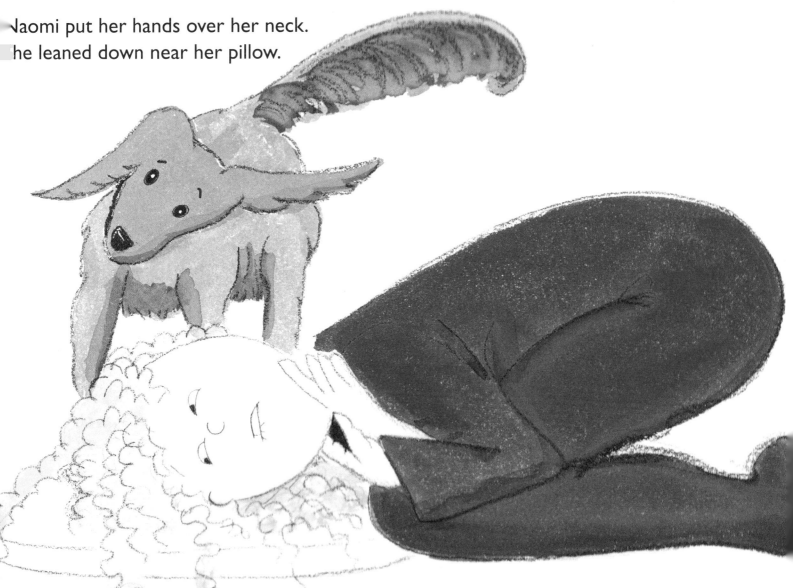

She whispered, "Excuse me, alligator. Do you want to bite my neck?"
She put her ear on her pillow and listened.
"She doesn't want to bite my neck," Naomi told her mom and dad.

"Does she want to bite your bum?" asked her dad.
"Maybe she wants to bite—"

Naomi gave him her super laser-eyes.
She said, "This is serious."

"You could ask the alligator what she wants," said Naomi's mom.

Naomi whispered into the pillow.
She put her ear down close to it.
She sat up. She said, "The alligator needs to talk to me.
We can all go back to bed."

Naomi and the alligator talked about scary things.
The alligator said, "I'm afraid of hunters!"
Naomi said, "I'm not afraid of you anymore.
Now I'm just afraid to take the training wheels off my bike."
"Me too," said the alligator.

In the morning, Naomi's mom and dad asked about the alligator. Naomi said, "I'm thinking about taking the training wheels off my bike."

Naomi ate some cereal and said,
"Sometimes you've got to listen to the alligator in your pillow."

"**Me too,**" said the alligator.

Talking with Children About Fear

Not all children discover an alligator in their pillow. Some children never wake with nighttime fears. But all children have fears of things real and imagined from time to time. So do most adults.

Here are some questions to help adults wonder with children about fear. This list gives you a variety of questions to help you begin to explore children's fears (and maybe your own) from a number of perspectives. Start with the simpler questions as a way of moving toward deeper feelings. You may want to reflect on the more difficult questions on your own first. You don't have to have all the answers! By asking "wonder" questions you can model that there may be many "right" answers and invite imaginative, playful responses.

The main things you need to remember are to keep the questions open and not to judge or dismiss children's responses. As they respond to the wondering questions, you can simply reply with things like: "Hmmmm…," or "I wonder about that too." Or paraphrase what the child says: "You wonder if the alligator's name is Allison."

- I wonder if the alligator has a name?
- I wonder what the alligator was doing in Naomi's pillow?
- I wonder how the alligator got into her pillow?
- I wonder what the alligator might really be?
- I wonder what Naomi and the alligator talked about?
- I wonder if you are sometimes afraid?
- I wonder what you do when you are afraid?
- I wonder who you would talk to when you are afraid?